THE JERSEY DEVIL

James F. McCloy
Ray Miller, Jr.

THE
JERSEY
DEVIL

THE MIDDLE ATLANTIC PRESS
Moorestown, New Jersey

THE JERSEY DEVIL

A MIDDLE ATLANTIC PRESS BOOK

Copyright © 1976 by James F. McCloy and Ray Miller, Jr.
Manufactured in the United States of America
Library of Congress Catalog Card Number 75-32056
ISBN 0-912608-11-0

Fourteenth printing, 1999

Maps, chapter openings, and illustrations on pp.48 and 53 by William Sauts Block

Title page and photos on pp. 17, 19, and 86 by William F. Augustine, courtesy of Rutgers University Library

The Middle Atlantic Press
10 Twosome Drive
P.O. Box 600
Moorestown, NJ 08057

For Ginger, Karen, and David
J. M.

For my mother and father
R. M., Jr.

CONTENTS

PREFACE

The Jersey Devil is a creature of folklore. For generations, south Jerseyites have been familiar with the legend of a mysterious monster that haunts the remote woods and swamps of that region. The dates, descriptions, and incidents of its history are often subject to controversy, and it even goes by two names. Although it is more commonly known as the Jersey Devil, there is an emphatic minority which insists that it be called the Leeds Devil, on account of one of its supposed birth places in Leeds Point, New Jersey.

As native Jerseyites, the authors frequently have heard tales of the Jersey Devil. This mysterious creature has fascinated us both, and several years ago some casual discussions about the legend led us to a collaboration in this work.

For reasons of style, we have attempted to focus on the essential points of the Jersey Devil's history and meaning. This has required the omission of many accounts of its sighting, particularly in January, 1909. In this instance, a comprehensive treatment would have struck most readers as repetitive. However, for those who wish to pursue the Jersey Devil further, we have provided a bibliography at the end of this book.

It would be impossible to thank all the people who assisted or inspired the authors during the course of putting this book together, but we would like to make some specific acknowledgements.

First, we would like to thank Dr. Jeremiah J. Sullivan, one of the originators of this project, whose knowledge of folklore was an invaluable contribution. We also appreciate the assistance of Bill Reed of New Jersey Public Broadcasting, particularly for the transcript of his interview with Watson C. Buck; Clark L. Beck of the Rutgers University Library for help in locating William F. Augustine's photographs, the Rutgers University Library for kind permission to use them in this book, and Bill Augustine for valuable background information; Frances Shute and Edith Hoelle of the Gloucester County Historical Society; Alwina D. Bailey, Director of the Millville Public Library; Jim Albertson, of Mauricetown; Mary Hysler, of Leeds Point; Chief Louis Pozielli, Officer Charles Pelle, and Dispatcher Amos Featherer of the Gibbstown (Greenwich Township) Police Department; Mary Lou Ponsell, Librarian of Wilmington College; Edward Jones, of Penns Grove; Jack E. Boucher, historian and photographer; Jerry and Nancy Bader; Champion Coles of Salem Community College; Francis A. Isaac, editor of *The Record,* Paulsboro; Mary F. Loughlin, Naval Historical Center, Department of the Navy; and our patient families for their tolerance and inspiration.

In addition, the Gloucester County Historical Society, Camden County Historical Society, Monmouth County Historical Association, New Jersey State Library, New Jersey Public Broadcasting, New Jersey Historical Society, Rutgers University Library, Ocean City Free Public Library, Free Library of Philadelphia, Bucks County Historical Society, University of Delaware Library, and Wilmington Institute Library, all provided assistance in the course of our research, for which we are most grateful.

THE JERSEY DEVIL

I. INTRODUCTION: The Home of the Jersey Devil

Slow-moving streams, stained orange from iron ore and cedar, slip through the stillness of the forest. Gnarled vines thickly blanket the occasional ruin long since abandoned to nature by man. In some areas not even ruins survive, nor any trace at all of former habitation.

In these woods there are places that are often no more than names of sandy crossroads in the wilderness. Among them are Sooy Place, Double Trouble, Hog Wallow, Ongs Hat, and Mary Ann Furnace. Their very sounds seem to underscore the area's remoteness.

Many of these names date back to colonial days, when settlers first tried farming the area. The sandy soil, dense with pine, oak and cedar, was unproductive for most types of cultivation. Some colonists moved on, taking with them harsh memories of the place they called the Pine Barrens.

This region extends across more than seventeen hundred square miles of southeastern New Jersey. Its desolation is amazing in this time and place. One can travel here for many miles and not encounter a single sign of modern civilization, yet the Pine Barrens lie within the most densely populated state in the nation, and in the heart of the great northeastern megalopolis.

It is an area unusual in a host of ways. Its vastness, its desolation in the midst of urban sprawl, its history, and even its geography run counter to common experience. For example, one section in the northern quarter, known as the Plains, proliferates in eerie forests of stunted trees that stretch as far as the eye can see. Although these dwarfs probably result from the combined effects of devastating forest fires and poor soil, the landscape looks so odd that thoughts of the supernatural almost invariably come to the mind of someone standing there.

The history of the region is atypical of most places in America. At a time when the nation was overwhelmingly agricultural, the Pine Barrens supported literally dozens of industrial communities. Furnaces and forges throughout the area turned out vital munitions for the American cause

in the Revolutionary War, wars with the Barbary pirates, and the War of 1812. They provided, as well, a variety of other iron goods for more peaceful uses.

Around the middle of the nineteenth century, a better grade of iron ore in the West brought the Pine Barrens' production into decline. There were efforts to intensify glass and paper making to keep the regional economy viable. These enterprises proved not very profitable, and chronic forest fires seemed symbolically to end chances of fully reviving the local economy.

Life for people in these Pine Barrens settlements had always been rugged, characteristically full of long hours and low pay. With the collapse of local industries, it became even worse. Many moved away, while those who remained behind sank even deeper into poverty. They left the crumbling towns and moved into the forests and swamps to eke out a subsistence. Disdained by their fellow citizens, these people of the Pine Barrens became known as "Pineys," a term which in later years became derogatory.

Their ancestry is still subject to speculation, but most regional historians believe that they probably descended from several groups: early settlers who attempted to farm the difficult, sandy soil or find industrial jobs; Hessians who chose to

remain in the newly-liberated nation, rather than return to Europe; and a remnant of part-Indians. The best known group of early settlers in the Pines were Tories, some of whom used the pretense of their loyalty to England to justify brigandage and a broad assortment of other illegalities.

Over the years, the residents of the Pines sank into incredible destitution. Some had nothing more for a home than a tent, or lean-to of sticks and branches. They used the natural resources of the area to keep alive. The seasonal jobs available—blueberry and cranberry picking, gathering laurel, holly, and pine cones for Christmas, along with such other subsistence jobs as collecting sphagnum moss, picking wild flowers, charcoal making, and cutting wood—were barely sufficient to sustain life.

It was not until the modern roadbuilding efforts of the twentieth century that the isolation of the Pine Barrens began to be broached. More accessible routes tended to foster movement to more prosperous areas and the jobs they offered. From an economic viewpoint, the lot of the people of the Pines began to improve. But the oldtimers, and some of the young people, watched in dismay as modern civilization nibbled away the edges of their extraordinary wilderness.

It is from this anomalous region that word first filtered out about the periodic forays of a strange creature. For two hundred and forty years, countless stories of it have circulated throughout south Jersey, passed on from one generation to the next. The details vary, since each time a story is told it is subject to being enriched by the teller. But constant through the changing fortunes of the residents of the Pine Barrens is the legend of a creature which has regularly terrorized communities in south Jersey and eastern Pennsylvania, and then returned to its lair somewhere in the Pine Barrens.

This is the Jersey Devil.

II. THE JERSEY DEVIL IS BORN

The most widely-held belief about the origin of the Jersey Devil is that a woman known only as Mother Leeds was the unfortunate bearer of a diabolic child. Struggling to survive with twelve children, the hapless woman became distraught when she realized that yet another addition to her overburdened family was on the way. Cursing her hopelessness, she cried out in disgust, "I am tired of children! Let it be a devil!"

Other tales give the child's birth order as sixth, eighth, tenth, or twelfth, but the most prevalent is the unlucky thirteenth.

Some say that this cursed being was born horribly deformed, while others say it was natural at birth and afterward took on fiendish characteristics. Then, according to some accounts, Mother Leeds confined it in the attic, or the cellar, for a number of years until it made its escape up the chimney, or out the cellar door, during a raging storm. Curiously little is said of Mr. Leeds at any point, although some people talk of a horned being secretly visiting the unfortunate mother.

The story of one of the earliest birth dates is among the most graphic. In this version, a violent thunderstorm swept in from the Pine Barrens across Burlington, New Jersey, one dark night in 1735, as Mrs. Leeds lay in labor, attended to by a group of old women from the community.

The candle-lit room was pervaded by a mood of uneasiness, for Mother Leeds was the subject of rumors that, despite her Quaker beliefs, she had indulged in sorcery. The women smiled, perhaps a little in relief, as a handsome boy child was delivered and placed in his mother's arms.

Suddenly, as they watched in frozen horror, the child began to be transformed. Human features disappeared. The body elongated tremendously, forming into a long, serpentine shape. Hooves replaced the feet. Its pink, chubby baby face coarsened into a long, bony structure of a horse's head. Bat wings sprung from its shoulder blades. Finally, it arose from the bed, larger and more powerful than a fully-grown man. The women stood transfixed in shock and terror.

Then the silence was broken by the monster's rasping snarls, as he curled his forked, thick tail and proceeded to beat everyone in the room, including Mother Leeds. With an ear-piercing bellow, and flapping his huge wings, he shot rapidly up the chimney and out into the night.

According to this account, several sleeping children were the Jersey Devil's first worldly meal. Other versions say that his first meal consisted of the entire Leeds family.

For the next few years the area was so plagued by periodic visitations of this creature that in the 1740s a brave clergyman exorcised the Jersey Devil with bell, book, and candle. The exorcism was supposed to last for one hundred years, and although the Devil did not remain completely absent during this period, south Jerseyites were particularly uneasy in 1840, their ancestors having warned them to be prepared. He did reappear that year, on schedule.

Another origin of the Jersey Devil is traced to the time of the American Revolution. This account, like many others of the Jersey Devil's birth, cites as the birthplace Leeds Point, a marshy and wooded section of land located between the Pine Barrens and the Atlantic Ocean, in that part of old Gloucester County that is now Atlantic County.

With American privateers operating in the area, and the furnaces at Batsto producing iron, the British decided to move against the vicinity. The result was the Battle of Chestnut Neck in

1778. It was around this time that a lonely Leeds Point girl fell in love with a British soldier. Townsfolk said the girl was cursed for this act of treason, and gave birth to the Leeds Devil.

A different version holds that the Jersey Devil was the punishment for the Leeds's mistreatment of a minister. The wronged clergyman foretold the Devil's birth as retribution.

Some attribute the legend to John Vliet of Vienna, New Jersey. In October of 1830, Vliet obtained some sort of mask with which to entertain his children. With Halloween approaching, the act increased in popularity in the neighborhood, and grew to be ritualized into the legend of the Jersey Devil.

One rendition of the Devil's origin is associated with a gypsy curse. Around 1850, a young south Jersey girl was frightened by a passing gypsy who had requested food. Because she refused the stranger sustenance, the gypsy cursed her. The whole episode was forgotten until the birth of her first child, which turned out to be the Jersey Devil. The Devil soon fled into the Pine Barrens, and was first seen around Leeds Point. His frequent visits there, so this story goes, led to his being called the Leeds Devil.

The glass-producing community of Estellville, Atlantic County, lays claim to being the birth site, in about 1855.

The Jersey Devil is Born

And around 1887, a Mrs. McCormack of Goshen, Cape May County, age eighty-four at the
time, asserted that she was personally acquainted
with Mrs. Leeds. Mrs. McCormack revealed that
the curse was put on the unwanted child by Mrs.
Leeds herself. Mrs. McCormack stated that both
the mother and the attending nurse provided all
the details. The new arrival was normal at birth,
but almost immediately metamorphosed into the
familiar demonic shape, and then departed out the
window. However, reported Alfred Heston in his
book *Jersey Waggon Jaunts,* every day the Devil
revisited Mrs. Leeds to sit in his favorite spot on
her backyard fence. Mrs. Leeds, afraid to venture
out to feed her strange child, remained inside the
house and tried to frighten it away by "shooing" at
it. Finally, the Leeds Devil got the message, and
never again returned to its homestead.

The late Rev. Henry Charlton Beck, renowned
New Jersey antiquarian, encountered many stories
of the Jersey Devil on his frequent visits to the
Pine Barrens, which he included in his book *Jersey Genesis.* Mrs. Carrie Bowen, of Leeds Point,
showed Beck what was supposed to be the exact
location of the Devil's birth. She took him down
one of the many roads that crisscross through the
area, through dense underbrush, and pointed to
brick and wood debris that was strewn about. Mrs.
Bowen asserted that a Mrs. Shourds, not a Mrs.

Leeds, had given birth to the baby Devil.

The details of this version are similar to the other accounts. Mrs. Shourds also hoped that her next child would be a devil, which wish came to pass. As her child grew, it became even more grotesque. One eerie night, as a dense fog moved across Leeds Point from the sea, the child winged his way up the chimney, never to be seen again by the family.

Then again, Mrs. Georgiana Blake, of Pleasantville, informed Beck that the Jersey Devil had three birthplaces. One verified the story by Mrs. Bowen, while another placed the event in the 500 block of South Main Street in Pleasantville. The last location was in Estellville. Mrs. Blake added that the departing screams of the Jersey Devil as he left his childhood home are the same ones heard when he is making a reappearance. She noted that he appears every seven years, and always is a harbinger of evil.

A Mrs. Underhill of Lower Bank told Beck that the Jersey Devil really was born along the Mullica River. There, the Devil was the child of Jane Leeds Johnson and Jake Johnson, who lived in a house on Cale Cavileer's Lane. The Devil has often been seen there by many residents as he rushes along the tops of fences between the Underhill house and Leeds's Lane.

The Shourds house, Leeds Point, reputed birthplace of the Jersey Devil, as it looked in 1952. It is no longer standing. (Photo by William F. Augustine, courtesy of the Rutgers University Library.)

The precise origins of New Jersey's most famous otherworldly creature remain shrouded in ambiguity. But throughout the nineteenth century, tales of his exploits were commonplace. Crop failure, droughts, and cows not producing milk were said to be his doing. To satisfy his appetite for fish, the Jersey Devil either boiled streams with his fiery breath or deadened the water with the fetid smell of his breathing. He also blew the tops off trees, frightened man and beast, and pierced the still night air with awful screams. Some claim that the Jersey Devil appears every seven years and is the harbinger of evil. Although the seven-year cycle for his appearances does not always seem to be accurate, the Jersey Devil does seem to materialize before wars.

The Devil has taken a wide variety of forms, shapes, and sizes. Different descriptions are frequent. However, over the years one can see the same elements occuring again and again. His size varies from eighteen inches to twenty feet. He has the body of a kangaroo, the head of a dog, the face of a horse, the wings of a bat, the feet of a pig, and a forked tail.

Folklore and history intertwine around the Jersey Devil. His sightings are often linked to the eminent and the topical. He not only appears among local residents, but is associated with the world-famous as well.

The Jersey Devil is Born

Legend has it that Commodore Stephen Decatur, early nineteenth-century American naval hero, travelled to Hanover Iron Works in the Pines. A pragmatic military man, he wanted to make certain that the cannonballs being manufactured there were of proper quality for his use in fighting the Barbary Coast pirates. While testing shot on the firing range one day, Decatur observed a bizarre creature flapping its wings across the range. With precision, he sighted and then fired a cannonball directly through the Jersey Devil. All present were stunned that the gaping hole did not appear to affect the Devil in the least. He continued flying casually on his way.

Another reputed observer of the Pine Barrens' infamous resident was Joseph Bonaparte, former King of Spain and brother of Napoleon. Bonaparte lived on a vast estate in Bordentown from 1816 to 1839, and is reported to have seen the Devil while hunting game in the woods.

It is said that the infamous Captain Kidd buried some treasure along Barnegat Bay, some time before his execution in 1701, and in customary pirate fashion he beheaded one of his band so that the spirit of the former henchman would forever guard the prize. After years of loneliness, the headless pirate apparently struck up a friendship with the Jersey Devil, and the two could be seen late at night traversing the sands of the

Commodore Stephen Decatur, whose name is linked
by legend with the Jersey Devil's. (Courtesy of the
Department of the Navy.)

Atlantic shore, or moving through the marshes and woodlands of southern New Jersey. At other times, the Devil was seen with a pirate whose head was still intact.

The Jersey Devil seems also to have sought female companionship. The only one of his species, he befriended other unusual beings. He was seen with a beautiful golden-haired girl dressed in white, and around 1870 was reported to be cavorting at sea with a mermaid. He also was said to have spent many hours gazing out on Barnegat Bay looking for sinking ships to laugh at.

The Federal Writers' Project New Jersey *Guide,* written during a Democratic administration, claimed that the Jersey Devil had a ham and egg breakfast each morning with Judge French, a Republican. Although it is tempting to speculate, the political leanings of the Devil remain unknown.

The creature kept reappearing throughout the nineteenth century. An 1840 rampage resulted in the heavy loss of many chickens and sheep. The following year livestock once more were attacked, accompanied by chilling screams and strange tracks. Posses could not locate the culprit.

Fear of the Jersey Devil never left the Pine Barrens, as W. F. Mayer of New York found out in the fall of 1858. Near the Hanover Iron Works, where he was visiting, Mayer located about fifty poverty-stricken local residents who lived in tents and eked out a meager existence from the cranberry bogs, either by labor or by pilferage. He met with Hannah Butler, a toothless old woman, just as a storm came up. She replied to a statement about the storm with a look of concern saying, "Aye, is there!. . .and a storm like the one when I seed the Leeds Devil." A male companion advised her against talking about the Devil in fear that the beast might be listening. Such a comment, such a state of mind, were typical of the Devil-ridden Pine Barrens. Mayer commented, in an article in the *Atlantic Monthly,* that many Pines residents preferred not to venture out after dark.

In 1859, the Jersey Devil was seen in Haddonfield, and in Bridgeton during the winter of 1873-1874. In the 1880s, the Devil was reported to have "carried off anything that moved" in the Pine Barrens. In 1894, the Devil lurked about Smithville, Long Beach Island, Brigantine Beach, Leeds Point, and Haddonfield.

In 1899 the Jersey Devil raided Vincentown and Burrsville, and apparently winged his way northward, where he put in an appearance along the New Jersey-New York border. As reported years later in the *Rockland Independent,* George Saarosy, a businessman, claimed his sleep was disturbed for a number of nights by ungodly screams emanating from the vicinity of the Lawrence Street Bridge, over the Pascack River in Spring Valley, New York. Saarosy spotted the perpetrator, which resembled a flying serpent. Some who had heard of the Jersey Devil recognized his description, while others speculated that it was a crane. Many remembered visits by a strange creature to the area in previous years.

After Saarosy's sightings, others also began observing the mysterious Jersey Devil-flying serpent. A red rock at Hyenga Lake was the reputed locus for the sighting of an unusual creature that could fly, swim, and run like a deer. The Devil eventually headed back to its home state, leaving strange tracks in marshes along the way.

By 1900, the belief was strong among many in south Jersey that the Pine Barrens definitely contained an eerie denizen, some otherworldly, frightening creature, which periodically would spread calamity throughout the region. However, some thought the legend would soon be relegated to antiquity. Charles B. Skinner, prominent folklorist of the time, took a hard-headed (or optimistic) stance concerning the Jersey Devil in his book *American Myths and Legends*. "It is said that its life has nearly run its course," he wrote, "and with the advent of the new century many worshipful commoners of Jersey dismissed, for good and all, the fear of the monster from their mind."

How wrong he was soon would be proven.

III. PHENOMENAL WEEK: January, 1909

Not only had the Jersey Devil *not* disappeared with the start of the twentieth century, but his influence was to become even greater. Of the two hundred and forty years of this creature's existence, nothing approaches the magnitude of his appearances in at least thirty different towns in the third week of January, 1909. He emerged from his natural lair in the Pine Barrens and wandered throughout the Delaware Valley, sometimes intriguing and sometimes terrorizing the residents. Never before or since has his presence been seen and felt by so many.

During the week of January 16–23, thousands of people saw the Devil, or his footprints. Their descriptions of the monster on his travels varied: they called him "jabberwock," "kangaroo horse," "flying death," "kingowing," "woozlebug," "fly-

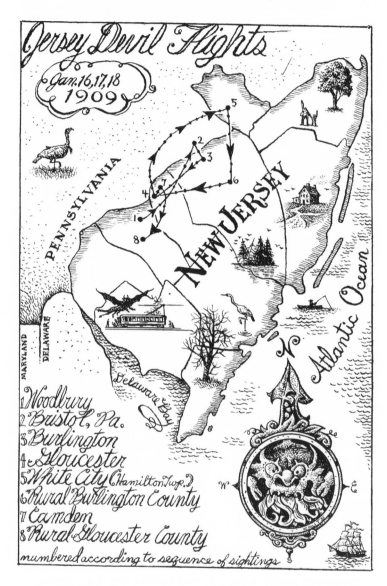

ing horse," "cowbird," "monster," "flying hoof," and "prehistoric lizard," among other things. Soon the population realized that all these beasts were in fact the Jersey Devil. As he swept through the area during this unprecedented week, schools and factories closed, people quaked in fear behind locked doors, posses scoured the region to no avail, and newspapers speculated on the shocking events.

SUNDAY

The curious week began somewhere between the late hours of Saturday, January 16, and the early morning hours of Sunday, January 17. In Woodbury, New Jersey, and in Bristol, Pennsylvania, different witnesses observed the Jersey Devil. A lone sighting was made in Woodbury, while several people encountered the Jersey Devil in Bristol. No one is certain which sighting was the first.

Saturday night, Thack Cozzens of Woodbury was leaving the Woodbury Hotel. As Cozzens recalled, "I heard a hissing and something white flew across the street. I saw two spots of phosphorus—the eyes of the beast. There was a white cloud, like escaping steam from an engine. It moved as fast as an auto."

The night was quiet as Bristol lay under a

39

blanket of snow. A cold wind blew in off the Delaware River. But at two A.M., three different people of Bristol were to think this anything but a peaceful evening.

Behind John McOwen's house on Bath Street was the Delaware Division Canal. He was awakened from a sound sleep at two in the morning by the crying of his baby daughter. He went to her room to calm her, when he heard odd noises outside, near the canal. The noises "sounded like the scratching of a phonograph before the music begins, and yet it also had something of a whistle to it. You know how the factory whistle sounds? Well, it was something like that." McOwen went on to say, "I looked from the window and was astonished to see a large creature standing on the banks of the canal. It looked something like an eagle. . .and it hopped along the tow-path."

Patrolman James Sackville, making his rounds in the vicinity of Buckley Street, suddenly forgot the cold. Dogs were barking and howling, and he knew the anxiety that comes to policemen when facing some unknown danger. Instinctively, he turned. There in the darkness stood the Jersey Devil.

Officer Sackville, later Bristol's Chief of Police, seems to have seen the Devil more clearly than did Cozzens or McOwen. The beast was winged and hopped like a bird, but also had the features of some peculiar animal. Its voice was a horrible scream.

Sackville ran toward it and the creature hopped in retreat down the path, emitting its frightening cry. Sackville started firing his service revolver. At first, the creature flew close to the ground, and then soared upwards, out of sight.

At about the same time, E. W. Minster, the Postmaster of Bristol, saw the Jersey Devil. This is how he phrased it:

> I awoke about two o'clock in the morning. . .and finding myself unable to sleep, I arose and wet my head with cold water as a cure for insomnia.
>
> As I got up I heard an eerie, almost supernatural sound from the direction of the river. . .I looked out upon the Delaware and saw flying diagonally across what appeared to be a large crane, but which was emitting a glow like a fire-fly.
>
> Its head resembled that of a ram, with curled horns, and its long thick neck was thrust forward in flight. It had long thin wings and short legs, the front legs shorter than the hind. Again, it uttered its mournful and awful call—a combination of a squawk and a whistle, the beginning very high and piercing and ending very low and hoarse. . .

Minster must have seen the Jersey Devil eluding Sackville's shots.

Other Bristol residents found their yards covered with abnormal hoof-prints the following morning.

After leaving Bristol, the Jersey Devil flew directly across the Delaware to Burlington, New Jersey. For some reason, Burlington seems to have been a center of Devil activity for this astounding week. Sunday night, late, Joseph W. Lowden and his family, of High Street in the center of town, heard "noise, as of some heavy body trampling in the snow of the yard." The source of the din circled the house, and tried the back door.

The Jersey Devil's tracks were seen during different times on Sunday both south and north of Burlington City. Two muskrat trappers, Clarence B. Williams and Charles Stupenazy, saw hoof prints in the snow around White City, Sunday and Monday. They followed the tracks for about a mile, and then gave up. Williams said, "I have never saw anything like it before." To the south, James Fleson, a Gloucester City liveryman, found prints in eight different yards Sunday, one trail leading into Andy McHugh's junkyard. Mrs. Ed Shindle found hoofprints in her yard during this week, and declared, "It's a two-legged cow with wings."

MONDAY

When the Lowdens of Burlington saw their backyard Monday morning, they found tracks, but not human tracks. The snow was packed down next to their garbage can, the contents of which had been half-devoured. Actual panic gripped Burlington that day. Doors and windows were barred and bolted in fear of possible attack, and many people refused to leave their houses, especially after dark. Some claimed to have seen the "Flying Death" but, in very human fashion, refused to divulge their names or to discuss the matter, for fear of ridicule by skeptics. Many others found the mysterious footprints.

The tracks defied rational explanation. Hardly a backyard in Burlington was untouched by them. They seemed to climb trees, to skip from rooftop to rooftop, to lead into the street, only to vanish. They led across fields, over fences, into inaccessible places. They would appear for twenty yards or so, and then completely disappear. To add to the general mystery, the size of the tracks varied—some as large as horses' hooves, some three inches, or smaller.

The aggression that grows from fear was clearly manifested in the Burlington panic reaction to the Jersey Devil. Attempts to capture or to kill the creature were made, or vowed. Reports of tracks poured in from the rural communities of Burlington County: Columbus, Hedding, Kinkora, Rancocas, and elsewhere. In Jacksonville, a hunt for the Jersey Devil was organized. Curiously, dogs refused to follow the trail, turning away in fear, and the men fruitlessly followed the marks for four miles, when the trail suddenly disappeared. Farmers set out hundreds of steel traps, nervously hoping to snare their elusive, eerie quarry. They were not successful, although there are unsubstantiated reports that several Devil hunters were captured in this manner.

Philadelphia Press

Phenomenal Week: January, 1909

TUESDAY

On Tuesday, January 19, the Jersey Devil made his most vivid and lengthy appearance so far that week. One of the most detailed sightings occurs on this day. The creature was now not so precipitously avoiding human contact.

At two-thirty A.M., at the home of Mr. and Mrs. Nelson Evans, a Gloucester City paperhanger, of the two-hundred block of Mercer Street, strange noises awakened frightened witnesses to a vivid scene. Peering out of their bedroom window, the couple watched for a full ten minutes as the Jersey Devil cavorted before their eyes on the roof of their shed.

The ten harrowing minutes etched into the mind of paperhanger Evans a detailed impression of the Pine Barrens' most infamous specter:

> It was about three feet and a half high, with a head like a collie dog and a face like a horse. It had a long neck, wings about two feet long, and its back legs were like those of a crane, and it had horse's hooves. It walked on its back legs and held up two short front legs with paws on them. It didn't use the front legs at all while we were watching. My wife and I were scared, I tell you, but I managed to open the window and say, "Shoo!" and it turned around, barked at me, and flew away.

THE NEW JERSEY "WHAT-IS-IT," AS NELSON EVANS
SAYS HE SAW IT ON HIS SHED ROOF AT 2 A. M.

*Philadelphia
Evening Bulletin*

Mrs. Evans told basically the same story, adding the singular detail about the sound of the creature's wings: "It made no sounds at all until it began flapping its wings. Then it sounded s-zzz s-zzz s-zzz just like the muffled sound a woodsaw makes when it strikes a rotten place."

Yet another fruitless tracking of the Jersey Devil occured in the vicinity of Gloucester. Hank White and Tom Hamilton, professional muskrat hunters, trailed the creature for twenty miles. They were amazed to see the trail jump five-foot fences and squeeze under eight-inch spaces. White declared the Jersey Devil to be an "air hoss," similar to those he claimed were native to his home state of Georgia. White said he would not venture outside without a gun any more until clearly the Devil was gone.

Hoof-print sightings continued all over south Jersey. William Pine's daughter was carrying the dinner pail to her father in Camden when she saw strange tracks in the snow, and fell into a faint. She feared an impending attack. Her father and others examined the tracks, finding that they resembled those of a donkey, except with two limbs—one seeming to be larger than the other—which made it seem "obviously deformed." Other tracks turned up in the vicinity of Dialogue's Shipyard, Camden.

Elsewhere in the city, a sighting was made that described the Jersey Devil as "something like a "possum, the size of a dog," which "with a shrill bark, flapped its wings and made off in the air" when its observers attempted to move in for a closer look. From Swedesboro, the report came in that the Jersey Devil possessed antlers, and from Glassboro, that he had three toes and was dog-like.

WEDNESDAY

Early Wednesday morning, an unidentified Burlington policeman was witness to the Jersey Devil, which "had no teeth; its eyes were like blazing coals." These and "other terrifying attributes" made the policeman sure "that it is a Jabberwock." That same morning, in Pemberton, Reverend John Pursell said of the Jersey Devil, "never saw anything like it before."

Pursuits of the Devil again took place on this day. Haddonfield, New Jersey was the site of two search parties, one led by a Dr. Glover and the other by a Mr. Holloway. They found many tracks, but the trails always ended suddenly, when it appeared the creature had decided to take wing. Camden County Freeholder Samuel Wood was one of the many to observe the abundance of tracks. In nearby Collingswood, Station Agent Kirkwood led a posse intent on capture. They saw the Jersey Devil, but got no more than a fleeting glimpse as it headed northward toward Moorestown.

In the vicinity of Moorestown, John Smith, of Maple Shade, saw the Devil near Mount Carmel Cemetery. Bolder than some, Smith chased the creature until it disappeared into a nearby gravel pit.

Not far away, George Snyder was peacefully

JABBERWOCK IN MORTAL COMBAT

FEARSOME creature as depicted in modern literature, the counterpart of which, many say, is causing terror in portions of eastern Pennsylvania, South Jersey and Delaware. Its latest manifestation is recorded in a back yard of a downtown residence in this city yesterday afternoon, where its appearance frightened a woman into a swoon, probably the thoughtless trick of a practical joker.

Philadelphia Public Ledger

fishing when he was shocked out of his serenity by a hideous-looking creature. Both Smith and Snyder's testimony agree on the details of their eerie vision: "It was three feet high...long black hair over its entire body, arms and hands like a monkey, face like a dog, split hooves, and a tail a foot long."

Understandably enough, the Jersey Devil was the subject under discussion at the Wednesday night meeting of the Ananias Club of Woodbury. According to the *Phildelphia Public Ledger,* one unnamed member smirkingly "said he thought he saw it dancing a jig on the third rail and fly south."

A trolley-car, operated by Edward Davis, was passing through Springside, just south of Burlington City, late Wednesday night. Davis was astonished to see a strange shape skip across the trolley tracks in the line of the headlight, and then disappear in the shadows. Davis's later words echo many others of this week: "It looked like a winged kangaroo with a long neck."

Riverside, New Jersey was concerned with footprints made over a thirty-six hour period. The tracks were ubiquitous, especially near chicken coops, buildings, and even outhouses. Joseph Mans found the tracks surrounding the body of his dead puppy. Mans at first attributed the death to his enemies, because of recent court testimony. He said that the prowler wore small horse shoes on the bottom of his shoes, and "left tracks everywhere, including the rooftop." Justice Ziegler dispatched Officer Borton to investigate the incident. Soon Ziegler himself found footprints in his own backyard. With a judicial flair for evidence Justice Ziegler quickly made a half a dozen plaster casts of the 2½-by-1¼-inch prints, which had been made all through his yard in a series of straight lines. Crowds visited Ziegler's office to see the molds, and his home to behold the tracks. Most Riverside residents held that all this was the work of a "one-legged, one-footed" creature, and not the result of any human endeavor.

By this time, the Jersey Devil had not only been seen in south Jersey and eastern Pennsylvania, but reputedly had appeared as far south as Wilmington, Delaware, Maryland—and even California and Canada.

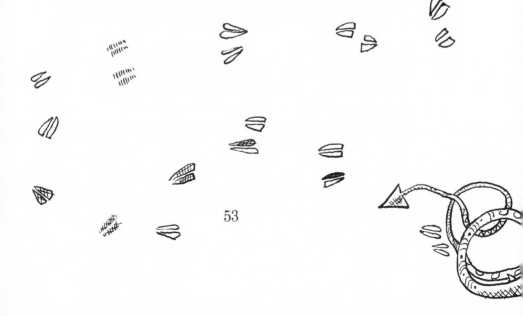

53

Jersey Devil Flights

Pennsylvania

New Jersey

Atlantic Ocean

Delaware Bay

January 20, 1909

N

1. *Camden*
2. *Haddon Heights*
3. *Trenton*
4. *Bridgeton*
5. *Millville*
6. *Burlington*
7. *Mount Holly*
8. *Leiperville, Pa.*
9. *Clayton*
10. *Pleasantville*
11. *Philadelphia, Pa.*
12. *Westville*
13. *West Collingswood*

numbered according to sequence of sightings

THURSDAY

Early Thursday morning, once again the Devil left his home in the Pines to begin the most harrowing day in his history as he rampaged through the Delaware Valley, leaving scores of citizens terrified and exhausted at the day's end.

The Black Hawk Social Club, in the seven-hundred block of Ferry Avenue in Camden, New Jersey, was having a meeting. Around one A.M. on Thursday, a Mr. Rouh was distracted by what he described as an "uncanny sound" at the back window. He turned to see a grisly uninvited guest staring at him through the panes. Mr. Rouh was terrified. Club members fled "in abject fear." Rouh, in desperate self-defense, seized a big club, and the Jersey Devil flew off emitting "blood-curdling sounds."

It must have been hovering in the Camden area. The Public Service Railway Trolley had pulled out of Clementon, heading in the direction of Camden about two A.M., and as it passed Haddon Heights, a passenger bellowed out, "There's that thing, take it away!" The frightened and curious passengers crowded to the windows to behold the now-infamous Jersey Devil. The trolley travelled some two hundred yards before it had to stop for a passenger, and as it stopped, the winged terror circled above, hissing violently.

Then, mercifully, the creature flew away.

Conductor Lewis Boeger recalled the apparition he beheld during the Haddon Heights incident:

> In general appearance it resembled a kangaroo. . .It has a long neck and from what glimpse I got of its head its features are hideous. It has wings of a fairly good size and of course in the darkness looked black. Its legs are long and somewhat slender and were held in just such a position as a swan's when it is flying. We all tried to get a look at its feet to see what shape they were but the darkness was too great. It looked to be about four feet high.

The Jersey Devil then went north, and alighted on the road from Trenton to Ewing, just opposite the Trenton driving park. It was early morning, and William Cromley was returning home from his job as doorkeeper at the Trent Theater in Trenton. His horse shied, panicked. Cromley jumped out of his buggy, to see "a sight that froze the blood in his veins and caused his hair to stand upright." Confronting him was a beast of fur and feathers, about the size of an average dog, with the face of a German Shepherd, from which glowered large, sparkling eyes. Tucking its two feet underneath, the monster hissed as it spread its wings and departed.

At about that time, Trenton City Councilman
E. P. Weeden was awakened from a sound sleep by
noises of something trying forcefully to enter his
door. Frightened, he flung open his second floor
window, heard the flapping of wings, and saw

Philadelphia Press

cloven hoof-prints impressed deep into the snow on
his roof. The Devil's footprints were also found
around the Arsenal in Trenton.

The behavior of Mrs. William Batten, of the
four hundred block of Center Street, was in-

dicative of the mood of the city. Having found footprints on her windowsills and doors, she barricaded herself in the house and announced that she would not venture out until certain that the Jersey Devil had gone.

Trolleys in Trenton and New Brunswick now had armed drivers to ward off any attacks.

So numerous were the tracks in Pitman that the next Sunday ministers in the town's churches noticed a large increase in attendance.

For a number of poultry farmers, Thursday daybreak was frighteningly unusual. Chickens had been missing from henhouses at widely scattered locations throughout the Delaware Valley for several nights. A new dimension was added to the woes of poultrymen in Bridgeton and Millville on this day when, after eerie cries were heard during the night, chickens were found dead with no marks on them. Farmers were unsure as to the cause—was it choking, or fright? They unanimously agreed that it was the work of the Jersey Devil, and were eager to see the monster captured or killed.

Tracks were so numerous on the snowy ground in Roebling that some declared it looked like a herd of shetland ponies had stampeded there in the dark.

More than just tracks were seen by Mrs.

Michael Ryan of Penn Street near York in Burlington that morning. It seemed to be a normal, cold, snowy day as she opened her shutters at six A.M. She heard a noise in the alley next to the house, and looked out to see what was the matter. She froze in fright. It had a peculiar shaped body and long bird-like legs, while its head looked like a horse. Its short wings seemed to be partly spread, and it was stooping as if about to leap.

Mrs. Ryan violently closed the windows and collapsed into a chair. As she retold it, "for some minutes I was so frightened I was unable to scream. My husband and son had already gone to work, and I was finally able to waken my youngest son, Edward, who was asleep upstairs."

Edward found no creature in the alley, and left to catch a train. As soon as the light was good enough, neighbors searched the place and observed small, pony-like prints leading to a fence. Mrs. Ryan and many neighbors were distraught for a considerable time thereafter. One Philadelphia newspaper reported that C. Rue Taylor, the mayor of Burlington, became so concerned over this latest Devil affair in his town that he ordered police "to keep a sharp lookout for the creature and to shoot it on sight."

In Leiperville, Pennsylvania, just north of Chester, Daniel Flynn was walking along Chester

Pike on the way to work. Suddenly he encountered an unexpected visitor from New Jersey.
He later explained, "it was coming out of a yard
when I first saw it and when the thing espied me it
ran up the pike on its hind legs faster than the
speed of an automobile."

Flynn evidently got a good look at the Devil.
He described it as, "the thing, which had skin like
an alligator, stood on its hind feet and was about
six feet tall."

The Jersey Devil also manifested himself in the
yards of two Mount Holly, New Jersey, residents
on Thursday. William Cronk saw it flying in his
yard—it resembled a crane. Job Shinn described it
as having "a horse-like head, long hind legs with
claws, and big wings." It stood erect and walked
on its hind legs, and "left tracks all over the yard."

There was a short-lived period of relief when
Councilman R. L. Campbell of Clayton, New
Jersey, erroneously reported the demise of the
Devil. Campbell's announcement was based on
the account of William Wasso, a track-walker on
the electric railway between Clayton and New-
field. Wasso was heading toward Clayton when he
spotted the Jersey Devil three hundred feet ahead
of him. The creature went up to sniff the third rail,
when his long, slimy tail touched it. There was a
puff of fire and smoke and a violent explosion

which melted the track for twenty feet in all directions. With no remnants of the creature left, Wasso concluded that the Jersey Devil had been annihilated.

Philadelphia Press

Another noteworthy report of injury to the Jersey Devil was turned in during this phenomenal week. Theodore D. Hackett, of the 20 block of North Ohio Avenue, Atlantic City, a lineman for the Delaware and Atlantic Telephone Company, provided information to the *Philadel-*

phia Record on how he rescued a besieged fellow
worker by shooting the Jersey Devil:

> In an isolated spot in the Jersey Pines,
> about five miles from Pleasantville, at a place
> known as Beaver Pond, one of the linemen,
> Howard Campbell, was detailed on a piece of
> work a little distance from the rest of the men
> on duty. After walking a little way into the
> woods, his attention was attracted by some-
> thing coming down the path toward him. He
> became so frightened by the unusual ap-
> pearance of the thing that he straightway
> made for the nearest telegraph pole. Letting
> out several yells for help and losing his wits
> entirely by the time he reached the top of the
> pole, Campbell threw himself out on the
> mass of wires between the two poles and was
> lying there helpless by the time the rest of the
> gang, including myself, had arrived.
>   Seeing the "Terror" on the pole, I raised
> my gun and fired. One shot broke a wing and
> it fell to the ground, uttering hideous
> screams; but before anyone could collect his
> wits the thing was up and off with long strides
> and a sort of hop, dragging one wing, and
> then disappearing into the pine thicket.
>   We got ropes and other tackle and helped
> Campbell down from his precarious position.
> As nearly as I can describe the terror, it had
> the head of a horse, the wings of a bat and a
> tail like a rat's, only longer.

Far from annihilated, or even wounded, the
Jersey Devil sailed over to the heart of south
Philadelphia, where he made one of his most vivid
and dramatic appearances. It all started when
Mrs. J. H. White, of the fifteen-hundred block of
Ellsworth Street, went out to her clothesline, having given her maid the day off. It was four o'clock
in the afternoon as she descended the back stairs.
There was a strange thing in the corner of her yard.
Only curious, she moved toward it. Instantly it
arose to a full six feet in height; she saw it clearly.
The body was covered with an alligator skin, and it
began spewing flames from its mouth. Mrs. White
screamed until her body shook, and then collapsed. Her husband, an insurance agent, ran
out the back door to see his wife on the ground, and
an unbelievable monster spurting flames from its
mouth standing nearby.

Mr. White could think only of defending his
unconscious wife. Bravely snatching up a clothes
prop, White ran at the beast, swinging his weapon.
The Devil scurried over the fence and into an alley
leading to Sixteenth Street, still shooting flames,
with White in pursuit. White shortly quit the
chase to return to his wife, whom he found still in a
swoon. He called the family doctor, who labored
for an hour in reviving Mrs. White from her terrifying experience.

A Sixteenth Street motorman, without knowing anything of the Whites's harrowing episode, reported almost having run over a grotesque, fire-breathing creature near Washington Avenue about the same time.

Other Philadelphians were to encounter the Jersey Devil on Thursday. William Becker of the Germantown section of the city claimed to have barraged the Devil with stones on Lime Kiln Pike. Martin Burns, along with several others, gawked at the Devil at Beach Street and Fairmount Avenue.

Going back across the Delaware River that Thursday, the Jersey Devil returned to his home state and again shattered the tranquility of a social club. Now it was a women's meeting in Westville. Two of the women let their glances wander from the proceedings out onto what might have been a peaceful, snowy field. There "it" was! The meeting broke up in haste, but not before a terror-stricken member reached for the telephone to call Harry Doughten. Rising to the occasion, Doughten quickly summoned up a small posse complete with dogs and guns, and resolved to track "it." They located and followed the distinct trail to the woods of Washington Park, but once again a posse failed to find its infamous quarry.

The Jersey Devil next confronted a group in

West Collingswood, and the event was reported by Alfred Heston in *Jersey Waggon Jaunts*. This was one of the few instances in which the Devil displayed himself to a large gathering at one time.

Philadelphia Press

Charles Klos and George Boggs were taking a leisurely stroll that evening down Grant Avenue, when they saw what at first appeared to be an ostrich perched on top of the roof of the fire chief's home. Concerned over the strange interloper, the two turned in a fire alarm. Soon the fire department arrived and turned a hose on the Devil. At first it fled the water by running down the street about one hundred and fifty feet. Then it turned, and to the panic of its tormentors charged at them. Sticks, stones, and other missiles had no effect on the rampant Devil, as it bore down upon the frightened crowd. Fortunately for them, the creature suddenly spread its wings and soared over them, disappearing into the night.

Leaving the routed West Collingswood firemen, the Jersey Devil travelled up Mount Ephraim Avenue and besieged the back yard of Mrs. Mary Sorbinski in south Camden. There too his behavior would be shocking and memorable. This was the only time a human witnessed the attack of the Jersey Devil upon another living thing.

It was now seven o'clock at night, already dark. Mrs. Sorbinski heard "a commotion" in her yard. Her dog was out there and, concerned, she hurried out to learn about his fate. She saw the animal in the "vise-like grip" of a "horrible monster!" She had carried a broom outside with her and she used it to flail at the creature in fear for her helpless pet. The Devil relinquished the dog, and emitting sounds which were the combination of the "hoot o:

an owl" and the "snarl of a hyena," flew directly toward Mrs. Sorbinski. At the last second he veered away, and over the fence.

The woman could control herself no longer. Carrying the wounded dog into the house, she succumbed to screaming in panic and shock. A large chunk had been torn from the dog's flesh. Neighbors thronged into the house. They found Mrs. Sorbinski "in a terrible state of agitation." Justice Wright of Eighth and Pine Streets was notified of a request for protection from the marauder. Patrolmen Thomas Cunningham and William Crouch of the Camden Police arrived at Mrs. Sorbinski's, where a crowd of over one hundred had gathered. Milling around in anxiety and curiosity, the people were suddenly electrified by piercing screams from atop the standpipe on Kaighn Hill. Running toward the hill, with the mob close behind, the two policemen "emptied their revolvers" in vain at the eerie specter. The Devil took to wing and disappeared into the dark eastern sky.

After this incident, the streets of Camden were deserted. Panic anew washed through the Delaware Valley.

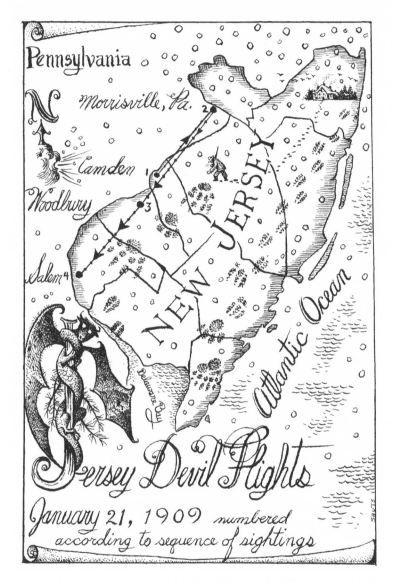

FRIDAY

Not at all daunted by the pistol shots in the night on Kaighn Hill, the Jersey Devil continued to lurk about the uneasy streets of Camden. At two o'clock on a cold Friday morning, January 22, he alighted on a roof top at the corner of Ferry Avenue and Vanhook Street. A Mrs. Stenburg sat up in bed. What was that on the roof? Hooves? Shaking her husband, she awoke him to the danger. He sprang from the bed, fetched his rifle, but was unable to get a shot off at the fleeting visitor.

Two hours later, Camden Policeman Louis Strehr observed what he called a "jabberwock" drinking water from a horse trough in front of John Carroll's saloon on Third Street. Patrolman Strehr described the creature as having the head and body of a kangaroo, "antlers something like a deer, and bat wings."

By sunrise Friday, the effects of the extraordinary scenes of the previous day and evening were being seen everywhere in all their emotional trauma. In the Mount Ephraim area many people refused to leave their homes even in broad daylight. The school in town closed that day, for lack of students. The absentee rate for many workers was quite high, and mills in Gloucester and Hainesport were forced to shut. A Camden theater canceled a performance.

The Jersey Devil remained out of sight until dusk. At that time two young women were returning home near Chester, Pennsylvania, when a strange noise from a stopped train frightened them. Out of a boxcar darted the Devil, sailing close by and disappearing.

About seven that evening, a report circulated that at last the Jersey Devil had been captured. C. C. Hilk, a saloonkeeper of Lamberton Street, Trenton, received a phone call that the Jersey Devil was locked in the barn on his farm across the Delaware River in Morrisville, Pennsylvania. The caller informed the astonished Hilk that the Devil had been riding atop a wagon driven into the barn by a farmhand. Several men then slammed the door shut, trapping the beast. A number of eager and curious rowed a boat across the Delaware to see the elusive creature. A search of the barn proved that the Jersey Devil had again mysteriously vanished.

The Devil departed the Trenton-Morrisville area, passing through Woodbury on its way south. Officer Samuel Merchant, sole member of the Woodbury police force, briefly observed the visitor. A sketch that he made of the sight corresponded to descriptions given by other citizens.

The creature continued south to Salem, where he remained Friday night. A Salem night watchman, Jacob Henderson, saw the unique being, and described it as having "wings and a tail." Unlike Mrs. Sorbinski's dog in Camden, Mrs. D. W. Brown's bulldog in Salem was successful in driving off the Devil from her backyard.

The terrifying forays ended as suddenly as they began. At this point the Jersey Devil returned to his home in the Pine Barrens, and appeared only once more in 1909. One day in late February, outside of Salem, Leslie Garrison on his way home at sunset crossed the stone bridge near Schultz's store, where he saw "a strange and very large and peculiar looking bird soaring above a clump of grown trees." Garrison stated that "it had legs five or six feet long, stretched horizontally and at the extremities were feet which resembled a man's." He added that "it must be the flying devil" that everyone had been talking about.

It took a generation to dim memories of the stunning events of this week in 1909. Up to this time, the Jersey Devil had been regarded as an old wives' tale by those living outside the Pine Barrens. But now, the entire Delaware Valley had been the scene for the legendary creature's rampages, major urban newspapers treated its appearance as front page news, and everyone speculated about it.

THE JERSEY DEVIL

Drawn by artist Ed Sheetz, this is probably the best-known "likeness" of the Jersey Devil. It appears on souvenir post-cards at the Historic Towne of Smithville, New Jersey, whose restaurants also feature a potent Jersey Devil cocktail.

IV. 1909 SEQUEL: Theories, Rewards, and Hoaxes

It was a peleosaurus cattelleya. It was a pterodactyl or an auropocladiuseta, or maybe even an asertoraskidimundiakins. Thus the scientific community in seriousness or in jest tried to come up with answers to this mysterious phenomenon during late January, 1909. Was the creature a prehistoric remnant that somehow had survived beyond its time? Was it mass hysteria? Or, was it Mrs. Leeds's infernal thirteenth child once again on the loose? Scientists offered a variety of empirical explanations. Most agreed that something did exist.

One tongue-in-cheek newspaper account was attributed to a Professor Breitkopf of the School of Science in Philadelphia. Breitkopf announced that the numerous tracks were made by prehistoric animals, obviously peleosaurus cattelleya of the Jurassic period. These beasts had survived in limestone caves which had sunk beneath the Gulf Stream. With trapped air, fresh water and food, the life cycle continued. Recent volcanic activity allowed them to escape their underground home and to swim to the shores of south Jersey. Breitkopf described peleosaurus as being twenty feet tall. They walked on their hind legs and used their membrane forelegs for flying. The professor advised that "no fear need be had of these beasts and anyone finding one . . . pen him up and feed him milk and fish."

Other reports had it that an expert from the Smithsonian Institution, who also held the theory about ancient creatures living in underground caverns, believed the Jersey Devil was a pterodactyl, a flying reptile from millions of years ago. Another report said that Samuel P. Langley, the famed pioneer aviator, upon hearing that the Jersey Devil had arrived in California, felt that it could fly the continent in a single night.

Three prominent New Jerseyites speculated about the Jersey Devil. J. K. Hewitt, a naturalist of the five hundred block of Chestnut Street in Camden, declared without doubt that the beast "was a jabberwock." Francis B. Lee, noted authority on the state, said that this was merely one of the Devil's periodic visits, and there was no need for alarm. Professor Leopold Bachman, a scientist from Griggstown, believed that it might be "the missing link."

A nonscientist, Mrs. Joseph Cassidy of Clayton, New Jersey discerned from both the noises and footprints that the recent events were caused by another invasion of the scrow-foot ducks. These large web-footed birds have no claws and had created confusion years before in Gloucester County. During that previous scare the ground also had been covered with snow. The ducks landed in the woods, and raised such a tumult that it terrified the surrounding neighborhood. A posse armed itself and marched to the edge of the woods, but dared not enter. At the top of their voices, its members yelled, "If you're the Devil, rattle your chains."

The Jersey Devil still eluded classification. To the Brooklyn Meteor Research Society it might be either a type of marsupial carnivore or a fissiped, both previously thought to be extinct. The Academy of Natural Science could find no record of any creature, living or dead, which resembled the Jersey Devil. Curator Witmer Stone volunteered, "There is no bird which would make such tracks in the snow, and there is no scientific record of such animals as have been described in newspapers." Several visitors to the Academy suggested, perhaps with tongue in cheek, that the

Jersey Devil was an auropocladiuseta or an aser-toraksidimundiakins.

The Philadelphia Zoo also became involved in the question. Zoo Superintendent Robert D. Carson announced, "I don't know what animal it is, but if it is captured and corresponds with the descriptions published, the Zoo will give $10,000 reward. It will be a valuable addition to our collection. Undoubtedly it could draw crowds to the garden and would be of educational value too—if it exists. But my private opinion is that it is going to be very hard to capture."

Geologist W. S. Reed, of Haddonfield, attributed the whole ongoing story of the Jersey Devil to "the mild but general idiocy on the part of the public," and then offered an elaborate explanation of the tracks. Reed believed that these markings were actually human footprints affected by the elements. He explained that the footprints left in the soft, dry snow were crystallized by subsequent rains which froze in the tracks. The freezing process caused the frozen snow to expand, thereby making the footprints appear much smaller than they originally were. This process, Reed claimed, also obscured the impressions of the middle of the shoe, and resulted in the curved "horse shoe" effect. Reed's theory did not deal with tracks located in inaccessible places, nor did

ANOTHER VIEW OF THE NEW JERSEY "WHAT-IS-IT"

Philadelphia
Public Ledger

DRAWN FROM A SALEM FARMER'S DESCRIPTION
This farmer says he saw the weird animal yesterday cavorting in his back yard, and that he hasn't tasted applejack since Christmas.

he attempt to give a detailed explanation of whatever it was that many people had seen and heard during that week.

Actually, a small number of the footprints might be attributed to those who sought to add excitement by planting false ones. G. W. Green, of Salem, admitted in the 1960s, many years after the events, that he had made some of these prints to create additional action. No doubt there were other pranksters, but still there is no logical explanation for the vast majority of the prints.

While much of the Delaware Valley was in fear, or disdain, of the recent diabolic events, there were those who sought to exploit the sensation for money and notoriety. With such potential for promotional opportunity, it was only a matter of time before ambitious showmen came along to take advantage of the situation. These entrepreneurs appeared in the persons of Jacob F. Hope and Norman Jefferies.

Hope was an animal trainer, and Jefferies the publicist, for T. F. Hopkins's Ninth and Arch Street Museum in Philadelphia. In order to bolster attendance, a story was concocted that Hope had had a mysterious creature in his possession, but that it had escaped two weeks previously—and this creature had been the cause of the turmoil throughout the area. Hope proclaimed that he was anxious to have his thing returned, as it was "the only rare Australian Vampire in captivity," before it escaped. So eager was he to recover his prize that he offered a $500 reward for its capture. He cautioned that his escaped charge presented a threat to both wildlife and pets.

Hope provided lurid detail in describing the habits of the fugitive. It was "carnivorous, with a huge appetite, feeding ravenously on rabbits, chickens and other small animals, rending them savagely with its terrible claws." It carried them beneath its bat-like wings until it chose to devour them. He had also seen the vampire tear a large cat "limb to limb."

As the story goes, Hope supposedly received word from George Hartzell of the twenty-five hundred block of Lee Street in Philadelphia, that the beast was streaking through the woods at the eastern end of Allegheny Avenue. Hartzell offered a $50 reward for the creature, which he clearly saw as a good investment in gaining $500 from Hope. Hope rallied a dozen highly skilled animal handlers, armed with "nets, javelins, marlin spikes, and cobblestones," and ventured into the woods. A "struggle" ensued, and the creature was finally subdued when one man with a net climbed the tree under which the Devil was standing his ground. While the party pelted the vampire with snowballs, the stalwart in the tree dropped the net.

A less exciting version of the capture appeared in a local newspaper. In this account, a box was opened and out meandered a harmless "Jersey Devil," which started peacefully grazing on some brown grass where the snow had melted. The handlers then "fell upon" the hapless animal and hauled it off for exhibition. Now the show was on!

Years later, Norman Jefferies confessed his role in the hoax. Jefferies was notorious for bizarre promotional escapades. One of his best known efforts was the marriage of Quasimodo, a noseless dwarf, to a beautiful girl in a public ceremony. The marriage was later annulled.

Jefferies's Jersey Devil charade was described by Watson C. Buck, a south Jersey oldtimer with vivid memories of the affair:

> When the hysteria built up, that was Jefferies's golden opportunity to cash in on the hoax. He went up to New York State, rented a large kangaroo from a friend, brought it to Philadelphia, and painted green stripes on it. The kangaroo licked his stripes and like to died. Then he tried another paint, which the kangaroo accepted, and he made a set of false wings, which the kangaroo promptly demolished. So he made another

9TH AND ARCH MUSEUM

T. F. HOPKINS................Manager

CAUGHT!!!
AND HERE!!!
ALIVE!!!

THE

LEEDS DEVIL

Captured Friday After a Terrific Struggle

EXHIBITED EXCLUSIVELY HERE AT
$1000.00 A WEEK.

The Fearful, Frightful,
Ferocious Monster Which
Has Been Terrorizing
Two States.

Swims! Flys! Gallops!

Exhibited Securely Chained
In a Massive Steel Cage.

A LIVING DRAGON

More Fearsome Than
the Fabled Monsters
of Mythology.
DON'T MISS THE
SIGHT OF A LIFETIME.

BIG STRING OF
SENSATIONS IN
CURIO HALL

THEATRE

GRAND CONTINUOUS VAUDEVILLE

10¢ ADMITS TO ALL

Philadelphia
Public Ledger

set, out of thin bronze this time, and covered it with rabbit fur.

Then to continue his hoax, he went to the Tenderloin, got fifteen or twenty roustabouts, dressed them in farmer's clothes, and took them, the kangaroo, pitchforks and nets to Huntington Park, which at the time was closed. It had a large fence around it, so people couldn't see what he was doing.

They took the kangaroo in there, and these "farmers" spread the nets and pitchforks and "captured" this monster so they could get a picture of it.

Jefferies then took the kangaroo in the cellar of the old Dime Museum, fixed the stage up, put gnawed bones on the floor, brought the kangaroo in, and he was ready for business. But the kangaroo wouldn't cooperate, so he stationed a boy holding a stick with a nail in it in back of the cage.

The audience was led in, the boy poked the kangaroo, and it jumped to the front of the cage, green whiskers flowing, bells ringing, and just for an instant he was seen. Then the curtain came down and Jefferies was ready for another batch of sightseers.

The Eleventh Street Opera House, between Chestnut and Market in Philadelphia, also announced the exhibit of a Jersey Devil. They offered a special bargain at the Wednesday and Saturday matinees, where, for only twenty-five cents, one

A Master Hoaxer Tells All!

The Philadelphian Who 'Invented' the Jersey Devil and Startled a Gullible Public With a Host of Fantastic Fakes at Last Reveals How He Did It.

By HARRY N. MOORE

"NO," said the rather small, neat man, selecting a cigarette, "you're wrong. People don't like to be fooled." He paused and struck a match. "What people like is to fool themselves."

The small man was not a professor of psychology. But he knew what he was talking about.

From actual experience he is one beyond most of the professors in the art of mass suggestion. For he has been the cause of millions of people fooling themselves. That is why he was a success in his work. Few press agents have achieved greater triumph than this man, Norman Jefferies, who now operates a well-known theatrical agency in Philadelphia's Real Estate Trust Building.

"It stands to reason that most people like to fool themselves," the former press agent continued. "Just consider how many of us go through life doing that very thing. We pride ourselves on having made a certain success in business. But if we carefully examine what we started out to do, our early ambitions and dreams, we find we are only kidding ourselves. We are comparative failures.

"Many men and women persuade themselves that they are in love. They are. They are in love with love, but not with the particular person to whom they fool themselves into believing they have given their hearts. They marry. And then they go on, trying to convince themselves that they are happy. Usually a month is inevitable.

"Then to prove his theory that people like to fool themselves, Norman Jefferies recalled two of his greatest coups. One was the famous Jersey Devil. The other was the exploitation of the *Gabof* mermaids.

"May the devil fly off with the baby," said a young woman in 1790, and the legend of the Jersey Devil was born—but it took the odd genius of Norman Jefferies to make the mythical monster famous.

escapis in the place. Jefferies passed on.

He wandered along Ninth street and

devil fly off with it," she said.

That night the child was born. But in the morning there was no trace of

it momentarily flew up the chimney with a whoop and disappeared.

Either version would have suited Jefferies equally well. In his office he artfully wove a newspaper story, dating it from a South Jersey town. The story read something like this:

"The Jersey Devil, which has not been seen in this locality since 1790, has reappeared. The monster was seen by Mrs. D. C. Bevs, wife of a worthy farmer near the barn. It approached her, but she escaped. Tracks of the devil were later examined and could not be identified with those of any known beast."

On the following day, Jefferies dispatched an employee to the town from which he had dated the dispatch, with instruction to mail it from there. It was addressed to the now defunct Philadelphia Press.

The Press accepted it in good faith and published it. The Associated Press picked up the item and broadcast it across the country. That was all for a day or two.

Just why that saw the devil, it is difficult to trace. But it is confidently stated that a certain married man, living in a South Jersey community, a night or two later, found himself staggering home from the local hotel in a battered condition. He had seen the devil. His face and hands were scratched. His clothing was torn.

But he knew that the brawl in which

the deadly vapors which were exhaled in a mixture of fire and smoke.

The devil was ubiquitous. He was seen all over the southern part of the State. He was seen in the rural parts of Pennsylvania, Delaware and Maryland, all on the same night.

A newspaper sent experts to examine the tracks and had plaster casts made. These were exhibited in the windows of the newspaper office. Works for demonology were in demand. Finally the learned professors were drawn into the discussion.

One who shall be nameless, but who was connected with the Smithsonian Institution, declared that the appearance of the monster bore out his long-cherished theory that there still existed in hidden caverns and caves, deep in the interior of the earth, survivors of those prehistoric animals the fossilized remains of which always in their size to a long article to debate the subject and added to the idea that the Jersey monster could be nothing other than a pterodactyl.

Under such influences the terror grew and spread. The whole district was in a panic. In south Jersey no one ventured out after nightfall. The churches could not hold evening services. Factories that were working double shifts, closed down at 5 P. M. Even Jefferies himself felt his story was becoming a boomerang, for the Broadway theater in Camden, now the Lyric, in which he held an interest, was obliged to close in-

[...] conclusion that the Jersey [...] taking into consideration the [...] on time between New Jersey [...] forests, could easily fly the [...] a night. The scoffers were [...]

Meanwhile what of Jefferies? [...] was almost in a state of panic in fear of the devil he had [...] full in fear of the consequences [...] wave of hysterical fear that [...] ing the country, to speak [...] most serious effect on nervous [...] persecuted. So he made for [...] and the spreading terror.

From a friend, a Professor [...] wards, of Buffalo, who was a [...] mal dealer, he hired a huge [...] garoo. The animal was [...] securely in the museum [...] den in the cellar. Jefferies [...] work.

First he painted the kangaroo [...] with bright stripes. But the [...] picked the paint and smelly [...] a paint expert Jefferies then [...] an oil paint which suited [...] sickness of the animal dea [...] Broadway theater in Camden, now [...] final climax, and the "panic s [...] spreading.

Jefferies then fashioned a [...] of wings. These were made [...] ome materials, but the kangaroo [...] from this because. The wing [...] fixed with a harness of rubb [...] painted like the body of the [...] Then green whiskers were [...] about the neck. Now all was [...]

The next day Jefferies ushered [...]

could see both the Jersey Devil and Dumont's Minstrels. All Jerseyites were invited, with a special emphasis on Woodbury people, who were told to "come quick."

The *Press* of Philadelphia added to the fun of bogus diabolism in the Sunday, January 24 edition. The paper carried a picture of what was reputed to be the Jersey Devil, but which really seemed to be the remnants of a taxidermist's shop. The Jersey Devil, which "possed" for the photograph, had a deer's head, a peculiar looking bird's body, and small elephant-like legs. They identified it as being either a "gollywog" or an "ornizalichtlyodalacta."

And so, the Delaware Valley reacted to the strange visitor in differing ways. Scientists profferred theories to explain it, promoters exploited it financially, some refused to recognize the whole thing, and many others spent the week in terror. To this day, no definitive explanation of the Jersey Devil has been made. Interestingly enough, in the years that have gone by since 1909, few of the many articles and parts of books that have been devoted to the Jersey Devil have dealt with this amazing week. In the final chapter, some possible explanations will be offered.

V. THE JERSEY DEVIL IN MODERN TIMES

Each year millions of visitors drive down the Garden State Parkway or the Atlantic City Expressway to the Jersey shore resorts. Most of them are oblivious to the seemingly endless tracts of forest they are passing through, and unaware of events that have transpired there.

Some south Jerseyites, however, still have somewhere in mind the hint of a belief that this region is not so empty and serene as it may seem. When they drive these highways, they take comfort from the yellow call boxes which turn up every mile or so, and they believe they know why those emergency phones are placed so closely together. It is not, they will tell you, just for assistance with automotive difficulties, but the possibility of something else out there in those woods.

For example, around 1927, a taxi driver on his

way to Salem had car trouble late one night. Something definitely came from the woods then. He alighted from his cab to fix a flat tire and he had just finished the job when his car began to shake violently back and forth. He looked up to see what was causing the shaking and saw "something that stood upright like a man but without clothing and covered with hair." Leaving the flat tire and jack behind in his flight, he drove full-speed into Salem, where he excitedly announced his encounter with the Jersey Devil. Edward R. Jones and Bill Reed, Salemites "having more nerve than sense," sped off in Jones's car to investigate. The taxi driver, however, saw fit to remain behind. The two found only the flat tire and the jack, but the Devil had slipped back into the surrounding darkness.

In the twentieth century, the Pine Barrens have been increasingly encroached upon by super-highways, the huge Fort Dix complex, housing developments, and even the possibility of a proposed super-jetport. The population of southern and central Jersey has grown so that its housing appetite has eaten away at the edges of the Barrens. Cement and tar cover an ever-increasing amount of the region each year. Enormous jets roar overhead on their way to McGuire Air Force Base or Philadelphia, booming through the calm of the long stretches of woods below. Despite these contemporary incursions, the spirit of the Jersey Devil still haunts the area. To date, there has never been a recurrence of the magnitude of that week in January of 1909, but his periodic forays, influences, scares, and sightings continue.

Two reports of the Jersey Devil's death in this century proved to be inconclusive. Around World War I, some type of a strange animal, reputedly the Jersey Devil, was killed and put on exhibition in Paterson. And in 1925, the *Woodbury Daily Times* carried an article about the supposed demise of the Jersey Devil. According to this account, William Hymer, of Greenwich Township, Gloucester County, found a strange beast consuming his chickens. After a half-mile chase, he caught the Devil, and the two engaged in a brawl. Hymer managed to shoot the culprit dead, and later proudly exhibited the carcass before the curious eyes of hundreds of visitors. He described it as being "as big as a grown Airedale with black fur resembling Astrakhan; having a kangaroo-fashioned hop; forequarters higher than its rear, which were always crouched; and hind feet of four webbed toes. Its eyes are still open and very yellow, and its jaw is neither dog, wolf, nor coyote. Its crushers in the lower jaws each have four

prongs into which the upper teeth fit perfectly."
Later efforts by the *Woodbury Daily Times* to
trace the incident found no records of any William
Hymer.

Woodbury Times

Throughout modern times, intermittent posses
to hunt the elusive being were formed, and they
made many fruitless quests. In the 1920s, there
were reports of a posse treeing the Jersey Devil in

Salem. A few years later, another posse chased what was said to be "a flying lion" in West Orange; they claimed to have captured one of its cubs. In 1932, there was a chase in Downingtown, Pennsylvania. In 1936, following a series of chilling screams and cries from the woods surrounding Woodstown, New Jersey, a heavily-armed posse combed the area.

Around 1930, Howard Marcey and John Huntzinger, of Erial, New Jersey beheld a particularly grotesque Jersey Devil. It had the "body of a man, head of a cow, large bat wings, big feet, and flew up in the air, and cut off the tops of trees." Some time after that, Marcey's twelve-year-old daughter Kathy, accompanied by Jacqueline Huntzinger, saw the same thing in the same spot.

Philip Smith saw the Jersey Devil strolling down the street in Woodstown in 1935. "Looked to me something like a giant police dog, kind of high in the back. He walked past the grocery store and disappeared." Smith, it is interesting to note, had a reputation for sobriety and honesty.

Just how pervasive the influence of the legend was in south Jersey is illustrated by the words of Walter Edge, twice Governor of New Jersey and United States Senator. Edge told Henry Charlton Beck, "When I was a boy down in Atlantic County, I was never threatened with the bogey man—no one was, down there. We were threatened with the Jersey Devil, morning, noon and night."

But not since 1909 had there occurred such a tumult as took place in Gibbstown in 1951.

JERSEY DEVIL "INVADES" GIBBSTOWN

The Record
Thursday, Nov. 22, 1951

A group of youngsters were at the Dupont Clubhouse at the edge of town. A ten-year-old boy was passing by a window when he glanced out. There was "The Thing" staring at him, with "blood coming out of its face!" He began screaming uncontrollably, "fell to the floor and his body was wracked by spasms." His screams were heard at the far end of town. The chaperone managed to calm him and the children went back to their games. The boy's brothers and the other children discounted his story. There it was again! This time, the police were called, and they searched the area without finding a trace of the ghastly interloper.

The next day, rumors circulated throughout the Gibbstown-Paulsboro area that the Jersey Devil had returned. That night, Ronald Jones, accompanied by a group of teenagers, hunted for the creature throughout the area. They heard "unearthly screams." Mrs. Elmer Clegg, and her sister, Mrs. William Weiser, joined Jones's group to discuss the frightening phenomenon. Another "shrill, unearthly scream" rang from the woods! "It sounded like some birds in the Philadelphia Zoo who are chained, or some animal in distress, but it was bloodcurdling and eerie."

Nearby, Jerry Ray was combing the area with a group of boys. Ray claimed that "it almost grabbed him," and added that "it had a wild look in its eyes."

The Gibbstown witnesses varied somewhat in their descriptions of the strange visitor. Some said it was seven feet tall, with an ugly face. One had it as half man, half beast. Others depicted it as a chunky man with a bestial face. Chief of Police Louis Sylvestro headed a search of the area "with floodlights and beat the bush." Reports had it that Chief Sylvestro was "weary from calls" of anguished residents.

Monday morning, the students in the Gibbstown schools were so excited that Principal Clarence Morgan called in Chief Sylvestro to aid in calming them. The chief placed signs on the outskirts of Gibbstown asserting that the Jersey Devil was a hoax, in an effort to keep out annoying flocks of tourists.

Around the same time, the Jersey Devil was ac-

Sergeant Louis Pozielli (now Chief) of the Greenwich Township Police Department, *left,* and Chief
Louis Sylvestro trying to discourage the influx of
curiosity-seekers in Gibbstown, 1951. (Photo by
William F. Augustine, courtesy of the Rutgers University Library.)

cused of attacking dogs in the vicinity of Jackson Mills. A terrier was torn to pieces, its hind legs eaten away by something having a "terrible yell," and two other dogs were badly mauled. One resident bravely decided to investigate the source of these terrible screams and maulings. He waited one night in the darkness, equipped for his defense with a broomstick. His flashlight caught sight of a being, for a fleeting moment, but then the light died. He described the creature as "sort of a wildcat, four feet tall, and long, and grayish."

In 1952, strange tracks appeared deep in the Pine Barrens at Whitesbog. F. A. Fralinger, the finder, notified the New Jersey State Police, who called in Wesley Gibbs, a State Game Warden. After an investigation, Gibbs stated that the tracks were the work of a prankster armed with a bear's foot mounted on a pole. Gibbs's conclusion proved correct; he later found the implement.

Deep in the Pine Barrens, at Hampton Furnace, foresters of the New Jersey Department of Conservation and Economic Development came upon some charred "eerie remains," in October, 1957, and their discovery prompted yet another obituary for the Devil. At the edge of a lonely cranberry bog, swept by fire the previous summer, they found scattered about a partial skeleton, claws, feathers, bone particles, and the hind legs of

Left to right: Wesley Gibbs, a State Game Warden, State Troopers Matthew Garbulenski and Charles Groves, and F. A. Fralinger examining the mysterious footprints, Whitesbog, 1952. (Photo by William F. Augustine, courtesy of the Rutgers University Library.)

A man's hand beside one of the Whitesbog foot-prints. (Photo by William F. Augustine, courtesy of the Rutgers University Library.)

some unidentifiable entity. While some believed the remains to be a hoax or a discarded trophy, others saw in this the end of the Jersey Devil.

Those who thought that peace had finally come to the remote areas of south Jersey were unduly optimistic. In 1959, a group of thirty gun-carrying boys was fined fifty dollars by a Wall Township judge, although they claimed to be out hunting "a monster." In 1960, weird cries and strange tracks once again began to terrorize people in Dorothy, near Mays Landing. Game Warden Joseph Gallo and State Game Trapper Carlton Adams were called to the scene. The official explanation was that the cries were caused by owls and hawks, and the tracks came from the hopping feet of a large rabbit—but local residents suspected otherwise. The officials agreed to set out traps and to remain in the area overnight, in an effort to calm the people.

Also in 1960, two substantial rewards were offered for the Jersey Devil. The Broadway Improvement Association of Camden promised $10,000 for the capture of the Jersey Devil, and planned to construct a special zoo for the exhibit. Harry Hunt, of Hunt Brothers' Circus in Florence, topped this effort with a reward of $100,000 for the legendary beast, dead or alive, and he said "the Jersey Devil would be one of the hottest attractions since

Gargantua. He'd be worth a million dollars at the box office." Hunt elaborated that truly "The Greatest Show on Earth" would be the Jersey Devil exhibited on the same bill with the Abominable Snowman.

Nineteen sixty-three saw yet another hunt for the Devil. Five young men combed the woods around Lake Atsion, not far from Batsto, one of the creature's favorite haunts. There they found tracks eleven inches long, and heard screams "like a pack of wild dogs," and "like the crazy screams of some cult worship."

The last visit attributed to the Jersey Devil was an extraordinary mangling of dogs and livestock near the Mullica River in April, 1966, when Steven Silkotch found his poultry farm ravaged by a ghastly night intruder. To his astonishment, he found strewn about and cruelly mauled the carcasses of thirty-one ducks, three geese, four cats, and two large dogs, one of which was a ninety-pound German Shepherd. The unfortunate Shepherd's thick collar was chewed to pieces, and his body dragged a quarter of a mile from the scene of the attack.

New Jersey State Police from the Tuckerton Barracks were assigned to the case. Trooper Al Potter came upon tracks larger than a human hand, but the tracks were not amenable to plaster casts because of wet ground. They led into the woods along the Mullica, those same woods which so often before have seen mysterious prints.

Wildcats, bears, supernaturally-large raccoons, were all suggested as the midnight perpetrator, but people in the Pine Barrens once again had that sinking feeling, as they recalled the periodic forays of the Jersey Devil.

So quite recently, or so it seems, this legendary being has again disturbed the normal patterns of the region's life. There is no doubt that, if the past is any precedent, the Jersey Devil will continue to reappear for generations to come. It has been exorcised, electrocuted, shot, incinerated, declared dead officially, and scoffed at as sheer foolishness. These pronouncements have had an effect on some, but certainly not on the Jersey Devil, who apparently has disregarded them.

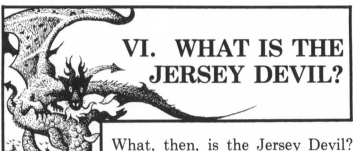

VI. WHAT IS THE JERSEY DEVIL?

What, then, is the Jersey Devil? There are as many different answers as there are versions of its birth. The only point which can be agreed upon is that the legend exists and the story has been passed on from generation to generation in south Jersey.

Jim Albertson, folksinger, puppeteer, and appreciator of the local south Jersey scene, has heard a number of stories about the Jersey Devil that paint him more as a prankster than an evil being. He tells about "somebody who did wrong to a neighbor, and a couple of days later found his outhouse turned upside down. By local accounts, it was the Jersey Devil exacting a little revenge for the wrongdoing."

Jim has observed that the more north of Leeds Point you go, the more benevolent the Jersey Devil becomes. This is fertile country for the traditional

101

"liar stories," in which a man will brag that he met the Jersey Devil on a road one night, arm wrestled with him, and whipped him so badly he hasn't shown his horny face since.

The Vietnamese War period was responsible for one of the most unusual local Devil beliefs. A bartender in New Gretna developed a theory that the Jersey Devil was an anti-war symbol. When the Devil would "pull something on you—a prank or something—it's because you were harboring violent feelings of some kind, and so he'd straighten you out."

Such legend aside, belief in the Jersey Devil is quite real, and based on records going back through the years detailing concrete occurrences of this being, times when he terrorized populations, ran down city streets and through lonely woods, when he attacked animals and was seen assuming a great variety of forms before many sorts and kinds of people. The Devil's activities have been witnessed by reliable people, including police, government officials, postmasters, businessmen, and many others whose integrity is beyond question.

Of course, south Jersey's having a mysterious creature is by no means unique. Many sparsely-populated regions around the world possess unusual denizens. Although the Loch Ness monster

'Where stunted pines of burned-over forest are revealed in darksome pools, the Jersey Devil lurks.' from Jersey Genesis by Henry Charlton Beck

This painting by an unknown artist hung for many years in a New Gretna tavern. It disappeared fairly recently. (Photo by William F. Augustine, courtesy of the Rutgers University Library.)

and the Abominable Snowman are the best-known examples, a whole variety of others exist, and they prove to be a quite infamous collection of local terrors.

The Fouke, Arkansas monster, which has been plodding around for less than two decades, is a relative newcomer. This fellow is large and hairy—and elusive. Many tales surrounding him, interestingly enough, sound similar to the exploits of the Jersey Devil. He has only been seen in fleeting glimpses; he frightens people; dogs refuse to track him. He gained nation-wide fame around 1973, when a movie, *The Legend of Boggy Hollow,* showed his "life story."

Another movie star is Bigfoot, of the American Northwest. Although belief in him may date back prior to the coming of the white man, in the Indian legend of the *Sasquatch,* interest in this ape-like creature is lively today. Two grants involving Bigfoot were awarded in 1974, a year in which he reportedly appeared forty times. The Louisa D. Carpenter family of Fort Lauderdale, Florida, provided $29,000 to the National Wildlife Federation to attempt his capture, and Peter Byrne received $7,000 from the Academy of Applied Science of Boston to establish a Bigfoot Information and Exhibition Center in The Dalles, Oregon. And in 1975, film producer David Wolpert offered

$10,000 for home movies showing Bigfoot.

How, really, did all these monsters come to be? South Jersey folklore has supplied us with a number of traditions of its Devil—the cursed thirteenth child, the curse of a gypsy, an act of treason, and the like—and the folklore and science of the world can be consulted to generate still others.

For example, if the kangaroo-like body, the bat wings, the dog or horse-like face and claws of the Jersey Devil seem to strike a familiar chord, this is quite understandable. Look at the facade of almost any gothic building! The ubiquitous gargoyles, strange blends of human and devil, are a traditional form of European devil whose history stretches back into antiquity. More precisely, they are demons.

Demons are usually seen throughout history as malignant spiritual beings either taking possession of humans, or materializing themselves in gargoyle-like forms. By all reports, these under-devils have performed similarly to the Jersey Devil.

It seems only natural that America's early European settlers would have brought the idea of demons over with them. These beliefs in the supernatural are evidenced in the well-known witchcraft epidemics of our early history.

What is the Jersey Devil?

Although the best-known witch scares were in seventeenth-century New England, they were also found in the Delaware Valley.

In 1730, for example, editor Benjamin Franklin of *The Pennsylvania Gazette* printed a report of a witchcraft trial near Mount Holly, New Jersey. Could this have had any influence on the story of the Jersey Devil's origin in nearby Burlington in 1735? It seems possible.

A corollary belief about the Jersey Devil would have it that Leeds Point's most infamous citizen was not so much a demon as The Devil himself, in one of his many guises. One belief concerning the Jersey Devil shows a diabolic origin in its assertion that he appears before wars—The Devil would fly about before a big, evil undertaking. It is perhaps unnerving to note that the Jersey Devil was seen on December 7, 1941, the day Pearl Harbor was bombed.

Some say that the Jersey Devil, like The Devil himself, is a personification of the abstract concept of evil. For generations, the Jersey Devil made it easier for people to deal with evil. Here, they thought, was an actual, rather than spiritual, being who could be blamed for a host of problems. So real was he that many thought they could precisely determine the date of his birth. The Jersey Devil, one could say, is Jersey's version of the centuries-old medieval tradition of The Devil. Deep in their minds, the many posses that pursued him throughout Jersey history must have cherished the thought that the world would be infinitely easier to live in if they could successfully confine or kill this Devil. After all, opportunities to slay evil do not arise that often. Crop failures would be fewer and fear would disappear from the quiet lanes of the Jersey pinelands at night.

Then again, perhaps much of this devil business is merely mass hysteria. Throughout the world, over a period of years, incidents of unusual behavior by large numbers of people have cropped up now and then. Europe, in the late fourteenth and early fifteenth centuries, experienced waves of mass hysteria. In France and the German states, people in many cities literally went berserk. They jumped up and down and raced through the streets, as they bellowed out the names of demons. This frenzy continued until they collapsed in complete exhaustion. In Italy, these actions were attributed to the bite of tarantulas. In the 1600s, another outbreak in Italy resulted in people screaming, ripping off their clothes, and whipping each other. Some theorists hold that these phenomena might have been caused by ergot in the wheat. Ergot, a sometimes deadly poison, has hallucinogenic effects similar to LSD. Whatever the causes, these mass events did take place.

Another similar wave occurred in an outbreak of hysterical biting, which swept through many convents in Western Europe in the fifteenth century. Frenzied nuns would bite one another, for some unknown and terrible reason.

But there are many contemporary examples. A number of high school students in Bellevue, Louisiana, in 1939 experienced fits of fainting and violent spastic seizures. This strange plague prevailed for half a year.

Mattoon, Illinois, was "visited" by the "phantom anaesthetist," in 1944. The supposed mysterious prowler sprayed about two dozen people with some sort of gas which caused paralysis and upset stomachs.

The early 1960s saw several episodes of mass hysteria in Uganda, Tanganyika. For a period of several weeks, many hundreds of people placed live chickens under their arms and proceeded to race about the streets, all for no apparent reason.

Booker T. Washington Junior High School in Baltimore achieved nationwide attention in 1968, when students believed that they were being overcome by gas. Fire department rescuers could find no trace of any gas, although the students displayed the symptoms of gas poisoning.

Over one hundred students and several

teachers caught an unknown malady at the Berry, Alabama, elementary school in 1973. Although many different symptoms were manifested, such as passing out and throwing up, the most common was scratching. Many scratched themselves until they bled. Despite the inability of health authorities to find a cause for the illnesses, school had to be closed about two weeks earlier than scheduled for summer vacation.

New Castle, Delaware, saw an interesting case of what to medical doctors was mass hysteria, but to others was the Holy Spirit. A gospel choir was heading from Wilmington to Salisbury, Maryland, when six of its members were overcome. They collapsed, had difficulty breathing, and had to be rushed by ambulance to a hospital. However, upon reaching the hospital they recovered, and continued on their journey.

Certainly, the question of mass hysteria can be posed regarding the 1909 week of terror. At this time also, people claimed to have seen a mysterious visitor and observed his singular activities. After initial appearances, more sightings were reported in an increasing crescendo of panic which ended as abruptly as it began. These events involved dozens of witnesses in countless localities. Perhaps it was hysteria after all.

Then too, some sightings of the Jersey Devil

might have had their origin in simple boredom, or the human urge to seek excitement. Anyone who has camped out in south Jersey and knows the legend has undoubtedly been warned to be on the lookout. A "Devil scare" often is standard procedure on the camping trips of young people in the Pines. The Gibbstown-Paulsboro affair of 1951 could be seen as an example of this desire for excitement. Here was an opportunity for people to gather, exchange gossip, and experience something out of the ordinary. To some of those who joined the many posses, an important motive was, no doubt, the chance to find adventure in their own backyard.

Jack E. Boucher, in his book *Absegami Yesteryear,* suggests that the Jersey Devil was actually a deformed human being, not a devil. According to this version, Mrs. Leeds gave birth to a cursed unwanted thirteenth child who proved to be deformed. Mother Leeds kept the unfortunate locked in the attic or cellar. Eventually she became very sick and was unable to provide the necessary care for the growing youth. Driven by hunger, the prisoner fled his home, never to return. The bitter fugitive took up residence in the surrounding swamps, and was accused of making raids on local farms. Any unexplainable and unpleasant incidents were also attributed to him.

Posses pursued the outcast through the woods and swamps, but failed to locate him. Boucher writes that, following a period of years, nothing more was heard from the elusive fugitive, but the story lived on as the Jersey Devil.

Possibly, whenever a retarded child was born deep in the Pine Barrens, he was labelled "another Jersey Devil." This could explain on naturalistic grounds the series of incidents extending through history far beyond the time span of one mortal.

There is another theory. When European settlers first pushed across the forests and marshes of colonial New Jersey, they encountered a strange bird whose ways could easily inspire a frightened imagination to conceive of it as demonic. This was the same bird that chased Jean Audubon into a river in violent reaction to its broken wing. Although the Sand Hill Crane in general did its best to avoid man, when confronted it would fight with incredible fury. Rumors had it that the bird had been known to drive its long bill into a man's brain through his eye.

The Sand Hill Crane weighs about twelve pounds, and is about four feet long, with a titanic wingspread of eighty inches. Once common in New Jersey, this bird dislikes man and now is usually found only in remote areas of the deep South. In addition to its size and ferocity, the crane showed other characteristics which could have startled those early Jerseyites. It possesses a chilling whoop for a voice, which can easily be heard at a great distance. These birds gathered in large numbers to engage in mating dances, during which they rapidly hopped huge distances. Seeing these crying, hopping, long-winged creatures, with their odd gyrations, could easily have led the colonists to supernatural explanations. The bird's eating habits also could have fueled the rise of devil stories, for the Sand Hill Crane has a passion for corn, potatoes, and eggs, which could cause damage to crops or raids on barnyards. Traditionally, the damage to farm crops had been blamed on the Jersey Devil.

The only certainty is that, by now, most people who live at Leeds Point are fed up with the Jersey Devil, because they are always being pestered by strangers knocking at their door and wanting to know about him. Mary Hysler, who lives just down the road from the remains of the Shourds house, says that people from Dorothy and Estellville claim the Devil too, and so far as she is concerned they are welcome to have him.

There is rarely a new moon around Leeds Point that does not cause a carload of Devil hunters to go thrashing around the woods behind Mary's house, starting the dogs barking in the middle of the night, and generally irritating everybody.

Mary herself doesn't believe there is a Jersey Devil, although she thinks, as do many others in the area, it is likely that Mrs. Leeds did have a deformed child. But, as she says, "it's just the natural thing for folks to explain away things they don't really understand by blaming it on the Jersey Devil."

Any of these explanations could be partially true, or wholly false. Such a matter seems almost incapable of direct proof. Some insist on their favorite explanation, or claim special knowledge of this subject, but not one of these theories or accounts can explain it all. The answer may lie in several of them.

Over the years, many have accepted the Jersey Devil's existence as fact. Others have derided and scoffed at it as baseless legend, and sometimes made those who believed in it objects of ridicule. But anyone who dares walk the lonely sand trails of the Pine Barrens, or the mist-shrouded marshes of the Atlantic shore, will find his eyes growing ever more alert, and feel just a suggestion of fear taking hold of him. It is hard to remain a skeptic alone in the curious New Jersey wilderness. An eerie presence moves there.

Major Recorded Sightings of the Jersey Devil

PENNSYLVANIA
NEW JERSEY
NEW YORK
Spring Valley

CANADA
CALIFORNIA
Paterson

Vienna

Somerville
New Brunswick

Freehold

Perrineville

White City
Reading
Morrisville
Trenton

Bordentown
Jackson
Point Pleasant

Kinkora
Roebling
Hedding
Philadelphia
Bristol
Florence
Burlington
Columbus
Conshohocken
Riverside
Jacksonville
Hanover
Rancocas
Barnegat
Rainesport
Mount Holly
Moorestown
Masonville
Pemberton
Downingtown
Camden
Vincentown
Pine Barrens
Gloucester City
Merchantville
Hampton
Surf City
Leiperville
Chester
West Collingswood
Clementon
Woodbury
Haddonfield
Mullica River Towns

Hammonton
Wilmington
Penns Grove
Glassboro
Mays Landing
Brigantine
Iona
MARYLAND
DELAWARE
Pleasantville
Salem
Vineland
Dorothy
Bridgeton
Millville

Goshen
Delaware Bay
Burleigh

Atlantic Ocean

● = 1909 Sightings
○ = Sightings at other times

N

BIBLIOGRAPHY

Books

Beck, Henry Charlton, *Jersey Genesis*. New Brunswick, New Jersey: Rutgers University Press, 1963.

Boucher, Jack E. *Absegami Yesteryear*. Somers Point, New Jersey: Atlantic County Historical Society, 1963.

Federal Writers' Project. *New Jersey: A Guide to its Past and Present*. New York: The Viking Press, 1939.

Heston Alfred. *Jersey Waggon Jaunts*. Atlantic County, New Jersey: Atlantic County Historical Society, 1926.

Jagendorf, M. J. *Upstate, Downstate*. New York: Vanguard Press, 1949.

MacDougall, Curtis. *Hoaxes*. New York: The Macmillan Company, 1940.

McPhee, John. *The Pine Barrens*. New York: Farrar, Straus, Giroux, 1968.

McMahon, William. *Historic Towne of Smithville*. Smithville, New Jersey: Historic Smithville Inn, 1967.

_____. *South Jersey Towns*. New Brunswick, New Jersey: Rutgers University Press, 1973.

Skinner, Charles. *American Myths and Legends*. Philadelphia: J. B. Lippincott, 1903.

Newspapers

Asbury Park Press
Atlantic City Press
Burlington County Herald
Camden Courier-Post
Camden Post-Telegram
Daily Republican (Doylestown, Pa.)
Evening Bulletin (Philadelphia, Pa.)

Bibliography

Gloucester County Democrat
New York Times
Newark News
Newark Star-Ledger
North American (Philadelphia, Pa.)
Philadelphia Inquirer
Philadelphia Press
Philadelphia Public-Ledger
The Record (Paulsboro, N.J.)
Rockland Independent (Nanuet, N.Y.)
Salem Standard and Jerseyman
Salem Sunbeam
Trenton Times
Trenton True American
Trentonian
Woodbury Daily Times

Other

Guttman, Howard M. "The Legend of the Jersey Devil." *The Crossroads.* vol. x, no. 4, 1973.

Halpert, Herbert. *Folktales and Legends from the New Jersey Pines: A Collection and A Study.* Ph.D. dissertation, Indiana University, 1948.

Leitch, Jackie, et. al. *The Cockpit,* February-May 1967, pp. 4-6.

Sullivan, Jeremiah J. and James F. McCloy. "The Jersey Devil's Finest Hour." *New York Folklore Quarterly,* vol. xxx, September 1974, pp. 231-238.

Index

Index

Index

Index

Index